Small Town Christmas

by

Nicole McCaffrey

For Mom & Dad —
With Love
Nic

Small Town Christmas

Cover Art by *R.J.Morris*

The Wild Rose Press
PO Box 706
Adams Basin, NY 14410-0706
Visit us at www.thewildrosepress.com

Publishing History
First Champagne Edition, November 2006

Published in the United States of America

Dedication

To Kath, my mentor, my friend, my hero. For all the "luuuv".

To D. For all the "magic," for all those early mornings (yawn) and for always being there. I couldn't have done it without you—and wouldn't want to. Love you, girl.

To Paty, for all the hand holding, support, friendship and encouragement. Love you, too!

To Kay and Meliss' for the Wednesday night "luuuv" --and for all the laughs.

And especially for R, who made it possible—and because 37 years is never too late to rediscover your sister.

One

Fat, wet snowflakes splattered the windshield as Holland McCall waited for the red light to change. Three turns of the darned thing and she still hadn't made it into the grocery store parking lot. She hated to drive in the snow. And only a fool would be caught dead anywhere near this place on the Wednesday before Thanksgiving.

Guess that makes me a fool.

The radio DJ announced a news break, and with a frustrated sigh, she jabbed the seek button on the car stereo. Officially on vacation from her job as the early morning newscaster in Syracuse, the last thing she wanted to listen to right now was world events. The scanner landed on "sounds of the season." She glared hard at the radio as "Let it Snow" poured merrily from the speakers.

"Bah friggin' humbug," she muttered, switching the thing off altogether.

It was twenty minutes before she found a spot at the far outer edge of the lot. As she stepped from the car, heavy snow began to pelt her head. She had showered at the gym before leaving Syracuse, and while her hair had air dried on the five hour drive to Castleford, the last thing she needed was to catch cold. With a foul-natured grumble, she reached into the back seat and found the hat her grandmother had knitted for her last year. It was brown and lopsided, but better than a bare head. She tugged it on and made her way inside.

Here, too, the holiday season had arrived with bells and whistles. While Bing Crosby crooned "White Christmas," she passed two women battling to the death over the last remaining shopping cart and felt a smug sense of gratification that she wasn't the only one in a rotten mood. But she wouldn't be staying long. A quick stop in the frozen food aisle, a few minutes in the express checkout, and she'd be on her way.

Thanksgiving was never her favorite holiday; she had dreaded it since she was a kid. Being forced to sit at a table surrounded by relatives she could barely pretend to tolerate, and listen while everyone bragged about their accomplishments—it was less a time for giving thanks and more an opportunity for boasting. She still didn't like it. Even though she had plenty to crow about. On the outside, at least.

As she rounded the corner to the freezer aisle, she saw, even from a distance, that the cases were empty. "Oh, no." She quickened her pace, as if getting there half a step sooner would change anything. It didn't. All that remained was one smashed up box way in the back. In desperation she went up on tip toe and reached for it; maybe it was salvageable.

She grasped the box at last and gave a little yelp of triumph—which quickly turned to a moan.

Blueberry? No one brought blueberry pie to Thanksgiving dinner. She heaved a sigh. She'd promised Mother she would bring the pie. Days—weeks, actually, of procrastinating and a busy work schedule had kept her from making good on the promise.

But there was only one kind of pie you brought to Thanksgiving dinner. Unless you wanted to look like a total idiot in front of people you really didn't want to see. Cousin Tiffany was making apple pie—undoubtedly with apples grown on a tree she'd planted herself. From a seed. But Holly was in charge of the pumpkin pie, and since her domestic skills were lacking she'd hoped to play it safe with Mrs. Smith's. No such luck.

Following the signs hanging from the ceiling, she headed for the baking supplies aisle. She would simply whip up a pie from canned pumpkin. How hard could it be? She might not be able to compare to the super moms of this world, like Cousin Tiffany, but she had spent many a winter afternoon in the kitchen with Gran baking cookies and cakes and all sorts of comfort food.

And she'd had the figure to show for it, she thought ruefully as she jostled her way through the crowd. But that had all changed. *She* had changed. Moved away from the small town to a big city. Lost weight in college instead of gained. Had blossomed in the anonymity a large city offered.

For some reason, coming back to the town she had grown up in always made her feel like a kid again. A fat, unattractive kid in coke bottle glasses

3

with mouse-poop-brown hair. She forced her chin a bit higher and squared her shoulders. She wasn't that girl anymore. She was a success story all on her own.

As she was about to turn down the main aisle, the sound of laughter reached her ears. Not just any laughter; the happy, belly giggles of a delighted child. Or two. She turned to see two cherub-faced cuties, dark hair pulled back in pony tails, giggling with delight as their father zoomed a shopping cart up and down the aisle. And then her gaze came to rest on their daddy.

"Oh, dear God, not now." Ducking down the nearest aisle, she hid there, heart racing as though she had just run a mile. The face was older, less boyish, but the smile was the same. And what her eyes might not have recognized at first, her heart certainly had.

As she stood there, too panicked to move, the three raced past her aisle. She gave a silent sigh of relief. Gran had told her Tucker Callahan moved back to town a few months ago. Divorced, she had made it a point of mentioning. Said he wanted his two little girls raised with small town values.

That's where you and I differ, Tucker. I want nothing to do with this place.

She shook off the momentary shock and glanced around to see if she was anywhere near her destination. Tugging the hat farther down her head in a pathetic attempt to remain invisible, she whipped out of her hiding place—the baby food aisle, of all places—and followed the signs to aisle

Eleven-A.

If the frozen pie section had looked like a Middle Eastern war zone, then the baking aisle was Ground Zero. For a brief moment, she wished she'd played football in high school. At the very least, attended a game. Because it was fourth down with no time outs left. Gearing up like a receiver intended for a Hail Mary pass, she focused her sites on the goal line—the lone, dented container of canned pumpkin. And went for it. Her fingertips were just about to brush the can when a gloved hand snatched it away.

Without so much as a backward glance, the other shopper plopped the can into her cart and shoved off. Frustrated but not finished, Holly stood there for a moment, mentally calculating the distance to the grocery store the next town over. But Castleford wasn't like Syracuse; there was only one grocery store in this town. Heck, it had been big news when they'd changed the flashing red light at the corner of Main Street to a full fledged three-cycle traffic light. She sighed. Next year, she'd buy the pie the first part of November. No, better still, the day after Halloween.

Halloween! Pumpkins. With a cry of triumph, she put her feet in motion. Sure, it might take half the night, but she could make a pie from scratch. She'd Google up a recipe once she got to Mom and Gran's house, tie on an apron and go for it.

Fighting her way back to the produce department was like swimming upstream. It took twice as long as it should have to wade through

5

shoppers fighting over bundles of celery and a near-empty bin of chestnuts. But luck was on her side. As she rounded the last aisle, she spied two orange blobs in a bin marked "pie pumpkins." The familiar sounds of a fast-moving cart and little-girl giggles bore down. She quickly turned her back as he raced past. Not that Tucker Callahan would recognize her. Or even remember her.

While he paused to look at the pumpkins, she felt a familiar pang of longing for the well-remembered sandy-brown hair, wide shoulders and long legs. One little girl stood in the back of the cart, a half naked Barbie doll dangling from her hand. "Pick that one, Daddy!"

He turned over a broad, denim-clad shoulder. "This one?"

She nodded, face animated with excitement.

The other girl, who appeared to be her twin, plucked a thumb from her mouth. "Are we gonna make a zack-o-lantern?"

A deep laugh preceded a gentle explanation about baking a pie. Her gaze wandered to the contents of the cart, a small turkey, a box of stuffing mix, eggs, milk, and several spice jars. The girl with the thumb in her mouth caught her watching and waved.

Holly offered a quick smile and turned away once again. Tucker plopped a pumpkin in the cart and moved on without noticing her. *Some things never change.*

The minute he left, she seized the remaining pumpkin from the bin. Like a linebacker with a

Thanksgiving game football, she clutched the pumpkin under one arm and dove back into the crowd. What were those ingredients again?

Eggs. Milk. Spices.

This was getting easier. All she had to do was follow the crowd. And sure enough, back in the baking aisle, they were all clustered around one area. The spices. She stood back, watching as shopper after shopper grabbed things like allspice, cloves, ginger, and cinnamon. Until her gaze happened across an ingenious little item on display in the center of the aisle. Pumpkin pie spice.

She snatched one of the tiny containers and half ran toward the dairy cases. *Eggs. Milk.* The handle of the cold half-gallon container dug into her fingers as she awkwardly juggled it along with the pumpkin, spice and her purse while trying to check the eggs as she had seen her mother do so many times. It was a ritual really, where she lifted the lid and wiggled each egg once or twice to be sure it wasn't stuck.

She shifted, hefted the milk a bit. The egg carton toppled from her hand. She let out a cry and tried to catch it, but it flopped upside down onto the floor. Other shoppers passing by flashed her the "you're such an amateur" look. Feeling like an idiot, she sheepishly reached for another carton of eggs while keeping an eye out for a store employee she could alert to the mess she'd made.

This time she set both the milk and the pumpkin on the floor and knelt beside them as she checked the eggs.

She had just lifted the lid when she heard it again. The giggles and shrieks of "Faster, Daddy!"

"Coming up on dairy," he called out, sounding like a tour guide, the cart barreling toward her. "To our left we have a lovely display of elbow macaroni at three boxes for a dollar. And to our right, the dairy case, where a dozen large grade A eggs are on special this week for—"

"Daddy, watch out!"

With a wild grope for the pumpkin, Holly tried to scramble to her feet. But she slipped on the broken eggs and went sprawling. The pumpkin rolled from her arms. She lunged for it once more, one eye on the cart coming at her like a runaway train. The carton of eggs tumbled from her lap. She darted out of the path just as Tucker spotted her. He tried to stop but skidded through the broken eggs with a "whoa" of surprise. She covered her eyes as the cart continued down the aisle

When she dared peer between her fingers, Tucker was sprawled on the floor, covered in raw egg up to his thigh. The cart had come to rest at the far end of the dairy cases. Two little girls laughed hysterically and chanted "Again, again!"

"Miss, are you all right?" Tucker scooted to his knees. "Did I hurt you?"

She put a hand to the floor to push to her feet; it came away wet, soaked from a puddle of milk. Raw egg and bits of shell covered her coat and jean-clad legs. It dawned on her the cold sensation beneath her wasn't the floor. It was spilled milk.

He rolled to sit up, made a grimace and pulled

out something from beneath him. Her pumpkin. "I believe this is yours."

Holly let out a little wail of dismay at the sight of the ruined vegetable.

"Can I at least help you up?" He rose to his feet and held out a hand.

She lifted a wet hand, grimaced, and spied the stringy orange goo and seeds clinging to his leg. So much for wanting to slip in and out of the store, for not wanting to see or be seen while in town. The absurdity of it all sent her into a fit of giggles.

"I suppose if you can laugh, that's a good thing." His face, alight with humor, suddenly sobered, and he crouched down in front of her. He plucked the hat from her head. "Holly McCall?"

Self-consciously, she raised a hand to her hair. A sticky egg-and-milk-coated hand, she realized belatedly. But her gaze was riveted on the fingers that still held her hat. Long, lean and calloused. A working man's hands. Her heart flipped over backward. She looked up at his face and took in the lines at the corners of his blue-green eyes, the denim jacket, the collar of a flannel shirt tucked over it. Not flannel in the icky beer-belly-and-pretzels way, but in the warm, inviting way. Oh, plenty about Tucker Callahan had changed. And yet he was exactly as she remembered him.

He smiled. "I haven't seen you—"

"Since graduation," she said, brushing bits of egg shell from her coat.

"Has it been that long?"

"Yes." She hated the bitter edge in her voice,

hated the memories that rushed over her. Soft, warm lips against hers. The heart-fluttering thrill of a requited crush.

The stinging pain of rejection.

She shook off a sudden stab of agony. No longer Fat Holly; she was Holland McCall, News Channel Eleven reporter on the fast track to bigger and better things. He was just some small town guy.

He rose and walked over to his grocery cart, and returned with a roll of paper towel. He tore it open and knelt down. "Let me help you clean up."

He began to dab at her coat, and she stiffened, resisting the urge to run off somewhere and cry. "I can do it." She took the toweling from him. A million times she had played out this moment in her mind, the surprise in his eyes when he saw her, the way she would ignore him as if he were nothing. She had never imagined their next meeting would come with her sprawled on the floor of a grocery store, covered in broken eggs, milk and overripe pumpkin.

"I guess I'll have to buy you a cup of coffee to make it up to you." He gave a half-smile she well remembered. Only it was better this time. A man at ease with himself and his world, an all around "nice guy."

A nice guy who had put her heart through a cross-cut shredder. And was probably too stupid to even realize it. "Never drink the stuff."

"Are you in town for the holiday?"

Irritated, with herself or him she wasn't sure,

she was about to give him a smart-mouthed "duh!" when she noticed the two little faces peering at them from the grocery cart. She'd know those blue-green eyes anywhere. Heck she could meet these kids on the street and know in a heartbeat they were Tucker's. "Y—yes."

"Good, then I can buy you a cup of whatever it is you drink."

"Diet soda," she murmured, pushing at last to her feet. The manager arrived a moment later and barked for "Jimmy" to come clean up the mess, then started cautioning folks to steer clear of the goo.

"Who's responsible for this?" he bellowed.

"I am."

Holly shot a look at Tucker, surprised to hear the same words come from his lips. She tossed her hair back and tried to compose herself as she rose to her feet. "I'll pay for it."

Like most men these days, the manager stammered and shifted his feet when she spoke to him. She'd never get used to that, never get used to the way men reacted to her now compared to the old days, when she had been invisible. "That's... not necessary, ma'am. As long as nobody got hurt."

"Just the pumpkin," Tucker offered.

"Oh no, my pumpkin," she cried, turning to look at the mess once again. The manager mumbled something about finding Jimmy and wandered off.

The sight of something orange in Tucker's cart caught her eye. "You still have one."

"One what?"

"Pumpkin. You could make it up to me by giving me that pumpkin."

He scraped a thumb across his chin and eyed her thoughtfully. "You want my pumpkin."

"Yes." She headed determinedly toward the cart.

"You would deny my girls pumpkin pie on Thanksgiving."

Her heart fell, and she stopped in mid step. "No, I suppose not. It's just... I really need a pumpkin pie."

One sandy brow quirked. "How bad do you want it?"

His suggestive tone had her swinging a gaze back to him. "Wh–what?"

"I didn't mean it like that." His boyish smile twisted her heart all over again. "Besides, you're probably married or involved with someone."

Was he fishing for information? That was interesting. Nonetheless, she had a pie to find. "How *did* you mean it?"

He stuffed a hand in his back pocket, then shifted and folded his arms over his chest. It amused her to think he was nervous around her when he never was before. Yet at the same time it irritated her. Hair artfully dyed just the right shade of platinum blonde, a nose job—something she had always regretted—to remove a bump from her nose, a figure that was maintained by little more than starvation and vigorous gym workouts, contact lenses, and the crush of her girlhood

12

dreams was falling all over himself.

So why didn't she feel victorious?

"I'd be willing to share my pie with you," he said, hands once again in his back pockets. "In exchange for a small-town Thanksgiving dinner."

"What?"

"No one does warmth and family like your grandma. And I'll bet my right arm she's cooking dinner tomorrow."

"I'm sure you have family expecting you." She started to turn away, resigned to taking the battered blueberry pie from the freezer case, if it was still there.

"Nope. I don't. The folks are out and about exploring the good ol' U.S. of A in their new RV, my brother is going to be with his wife's family and my ex is on her honeymoon."

She paused and looked over her shoulder at the sweet little-girl faces again.

Tucker gave her a sheepish grin. "It's just me and my girls for dinner. But I'd sure like to show them what a real family Thanksgiving is like."

"Are you looking for an invitation?"

"Are you looking for a pie?" He held up the pumpkin, bounced it in his hand a time or two like a basketball. "I should probably tell you, I make a mean pumpkin pie."

She narrowed her gaze on him. "Ever hear of extortion, Callahan?"

"Take it or leave it."

"Dinner's at three."

"Perfect. You can come by tonight and help

13

me bake the pie. The girls go to bed at eight, right after Spongebob."

Was he out of his mind? "I'll do no such—"

He tossed the pumpkin once more, meeting her stare with a gaze twinkling with mischief. "On second thought, maybe a quiet Thanksgiving alone with my daughters—"

"All right. All right. Where do you live?"

"My folks old place. Right across the street from your grandmother's house. Remember?"

"Yes," she grumbled. How could she forget? She'd spent half her adolescence sitting in her darkened bedroom, peering through the slats of the window blinds, hoping for a glimpse of him.

"Good. See you at eight then."

Two

Tucker set two wineglasses on the table, then reached to remove them. Should he? Damn, he hated second guessing himself. He set the glasses down with a thunk. She could have water or soda if she didn't drink wine. It was just a goblet.

He glanced at his watch, smoothed a hand over his hair, still damp from the quick shower he'd taken after settling the girls into bed.

From the kitchen came the smell of lemon chicken, the only thing he really knew how to cook. The water for the linguini was on, but he wouldn't cook the pasta until she actually arrived. If she did. Maybe she'd long since found another pie.

Nerves began to uncoil in his stomach like a ball of string. He hadn't dated since he and Kim separated two years ago. He didn't remember how to talk to women anymore, certainly not one who looked like Holly. The "Barbie lady," that was what the girls had called her. And she did sort of resemble the little plastic doll, in a perfect, not-quite-real sort of way. A far cry from the chubby girl who used to sit on her grandmother's front porch swing, pretending to be engrossed in a book, while he and his brothers played football in the street.

Those carefree days brought a smile to his face.

The smile faded as he remembered something else; his ex wife's parting words. *You wouldn't know romance if it bit you in the ass.* He didn't say the right things to women, didn't know all the fancy things they wanted to hear. Hell, eight years of marriage and he still couldn't tell when cuddling was just cuddling and when it was a prelude to sex. Even being a single parent to two little girls hadn't clued him in to the female psyche yet.

What could he say to Holly? Something nice, something about... her eyes. He snapped his fingers, that was it. Her eyes. They were...brown. A soft, dark brown. Kind of like... a dairy cow.

"Aw, geez." He smacked himself in the forehead. He couldn't say her eyes reminded him of a farm animal.

The doorbell rang, jarring him from his thoughts. She was here. And he still hadn't come up with something nice to say.

He opened the door and got the same gut-slamming sensation he'd gotten in the grocery store. He squelched a little "yowza" in the back of his brain as she stepped inside; reminding himself this was Holly McCall, not some sex siren. And even though she looked damn good, he hadn't invited her over here for *that*. Not that he'd turn her down if she offered.

"Sorry I'm late."

"No, you're right on time," he said, wincing at the lie. She was nearly fifteen minutes late, and

16

he had a feeling it was intentional. She'd let him squirm like a worm on a baited hook.

He reached for her jacket, catching a whiff of something soft and feminine as she slipped it off.

She stepped into the living room. He spied the table for two he'd set up near the fireplace. For a brief second he felt stupid for trying so hard, but then she smiled. "How lovely."

He sighed with relief. He'd worried the gesture was too much. And maybe it was, but for some reason he wanted to try. Tonight, for the first time in a long time, he really wanted to try to move on.

She fingered the lacy tablecloth with a murmur of appreciation. "Do we eat first or bake first?"

"Depends on how hungry you are. Would you care for a glass of wine?"

"Wine sounds great," she said, flashing a sparkling smile at him. He moved toward the kitchen, groping for something to say that wasn't meaningless small talk. She followed, glancing with polite interest around the kitchen as he rummaged through a drawer for the corkscrew.

"It's very cozy in here."

He glanced over his shoulder. "It looks the same as it always has." He hadn't even thought about changing the house; with the exception of the girls' rooms, it was the same way his mother had left it, right down to the furnishings.

A delicate pink flush stained her cheeks. "I've never been inside before."

"That doesn't seem possible." He located the cork screw at last. "Are you sure?"

"Uh huh." She took the lead while he carried the wine back out to the living room. She took a seat at the small table he'd set up, and he filled her glass before filling his own and sitting across from her. "I mean, I've been in the foyer a time or two, selling Girl Scout cookies or for Halloween. But I've never been inside."

Despite being a neighbor, Holly hadn't been in his crowd at school. The Callahan boys were athletic and well-liked, dated only the prettiest, most popular girls. Holly hadn't even been on the radar.

Something teased the edges of his brain, a memory she had probably long forgotten. But he was relieved to finally have a safe topic of conversation. "Hey, do you remember that time we teamed up for a science project? Whose class was that?" He snapped his fingers as the name eluded him.

"Mister Moore." For a brief second, her face froze. She replaced the expression with what he'd bet was the face she used when reporting bad news and rose to her feet. "I think I'm ready to bake." Wine glass in hand, she headed toward the kitchen.

He sat for a moment, stunned by her abrupt departure and mesmerized by the sight of her very shapely backside in a pair of snug-fitting black corduroys. Apparently he'd said the wrong thing, just as his ex had griped about. But damn if he could figure out what it was. She either didn't remember the science project or didn't want to be reminded.

Pushing to his feet, he followed and found her in the kitchen, frowning as she looked around. "Where is…?"

"It's in here," he said, slipping on an oven mitt and opening the door. "I think it's done." He pulled the tray with the pumpkins he'd already halved and cleaned from the oven and set them on a cooling rack near the stove.

She stepped closer to study them. "Can you really make a pie out of these?"

"Sure can. And it tastes better than canned or frozen."

"Well, right now it's my only option."

He grinned. "Desperate enough to put up with the likes of me for an evening?"

"I don't mean it to sound like that," she said. "I hardly know you, and you were nice enough to offer to share your pie with me."

"Well, I did almost turn you into road kill."

She smiled. "Okay then, what do we do, season these and put them in a crust?"

"Wait a minute—you were buying a pumpkin, don't you know how to bake a pumpkin pie?"

"I barely know how to bake the frozen kind. But there were none left."

He couldn't help a laugh. "That's pretty brave of you, being willing to try and bake one from scratch when you didn't know how."

"Nothing is impossible if you're willing to

learn." She set her glass down and pushed back the sleeves of her gray sweater. "Where do we start?"

"Why don't I mash this up and put it in a colander to drain while we eat?"

"You sound like a man who knows his way around a kitchen."

"Only by necessity. My ex-wife worked a lot of late nights. After a while even the kids got tired of mac and cheese and chicken nuggets."

"Your girls are lovely, by the way."

"Aspen and Sierra," he said, unable to help a smile at the thought of them. "They're great kids."

"So you're divorced."

"Yep." He forced himself to sound okay with it. He wasn't bitter and they struggled to keep things amicable, but it wasn't the way he'd imagined his girls would grow up. "How about you? Ever been married?"

"Only to my job."

"Your mother and grandmother tell me you're really making a name for yourself." He began to scoop the cooked pumpkin from the shell with a large spoon.

"I like to think so."

The words hung in the air, the silence that followed them awkward, as though they'd run out of conversation. He finally decided to ask the question foremost on his mind. "So are you seeing anyone?"

"No one special."

Unable to keep from grinning at that news, he met her gaze as he placed the mashed pumpkin in the colander. "Why not?"

"The last guy I was involved with... well, his definition of 'separated' vastly differed from mine."

He chuckled. "Well, I'm divorced for real. Nothing 'almost' or 'separated' about it. It was finalized a few months ago."

"I–I'm sorry, Tucker. Was she from around here?"

"New York." He reached to turn up the heat on the stove. "We met in college. I was impressed that she was from such a big city, she liked that I was a small town boy."

"But it didn't work out."

"Ultimately, we wanted different things." He picked up his wine glass, hoping a swig would wash down the sudden bitter taste in his mouth.

"Such as?" She stepped past him and took up the spoon, scraping the pumpkin from the other shell as he had. For a moment the warmth of her body, the sweet fragrant smell of her, the sight of her slender feminine hands as she worked stalled all coherent thought.

She looked up at him, brown eyes soft with interest. Oh yes, he remembered that look. He'd always been able to talk easily with Holly, had always had the sense she truly listened.

"Uh...well." He pulled in a deep breath. "All Kim was focused on was a bigger house, a newer car. Acquiring more stuff."

"And you don't like nice things?" She glanced up at him again, then brought her thumb to her mouth to suck off a bit of pumpkin that clung to it.

21

"Eeew, that's awful."

"It doesn't taste very good without the spices." He took up a kitchen towel to dab off her hand. He did it without thinking, capturing her hand in the towel. Something arced between them—or was it just him?

"I..." she said, her voice sounding hoarse.

He inched closer, unable to keep his gaze from slipping to her lips. "What?"

"I ...need my hand back to finish this."

His breath left him in a rush. He released her hand and stepped back. "Sorry about that."

She laughed and returned to the pumpkin. He retreated another few steps, using the excuse of pouring more wine to move away from her. Stupid. A woman like Holly would never be interested in a guy who came with a ready-made family and the baggage of a failed marriage. But for the first time in months, the nearness of a flesh and blood woman—and not someone in a men's magazine— had stirred him to an erection.

"So was that it?" she asked, sounding completely comfortable after their near encounter moments ago. "You and your wife differed over material things?"

"That was more or less the tip of the ice berg," he said, moving to turn up the heat under the pot of water simmering on the stove. "Then my dad had a heart attack and started talking about selling the business, selling the house, moving someplace warmer and taking it easy."

"I was sorry to hear about that. Is he all right

now?"

"He's doing great."

"Good." She set the colander to drain in the sink. She turned, picked up her wineglass and rested against the counter. "So did he end up selling?"

Tucker nodded. "To me."

Her face lit with interest. "You bought the family Christmas tree farm?"

"I did. But it was the last straw for my marriage. Kim wanted no part of it. She wasn't giving up her career to come live in the boonies and dig in the dirt."

"I'm so sorry."

He shrugged and dropped the linguini into the boiling water. "You know how things are around here these days. What hasn't been bought out by a super store will soon be closing its doors because of one. If I hadn't bought the land he'd have had to sell to some drugstore chain."

"Your family has raised and sold Christmas trees around here for as long as I remember."

"One hundred and fifty years," he admitted. "Isn't it funny how when we were kids all we could think of was getting out of here—but when you grow up you realize what you had?"

"I..." She looked away, raised her glass to her lips and took a hearty gulp.

He chuckled. "No regrets for you, huh?"

"Not even one."

He had no idea why the admission left him so disappointed.

****

"Are you sure I can't help you with the dishes?" Holly shrugged into her jacket and picked up her purse. The spicy aroma of pumpkin pie filled the air. They had just taken it from the oven, and now after a hearty dinner and three glasses of wine, she knew she should leave.

"Nah, I just put them in the dishwasher anyway." Hands in his pockets, Tucker shrugged, looking so adorably boyish her heart wanted to stop right there.

She untucked her hair from her jacket and flipped it over her shoulder. "Well, it was great catching up with you. I'll see you tomorrow at three?"

"Absolutely." He held open the front door. She stepped onto the porch, giving a little shiver as the chill of the night air met her.

"Good night."

He stepped onto the porch beside her. "I'm really glad you came by."

She smiled. "Me too." She started to step off the porch but he caught her arm. "Holly, you look…" he swallowed and seemed to search for a word. "Fantastic."

Right on top of the elation that he had said it, came the disappointment.

"Did I say something wrong?"

"No, I…" she glanced down at her feet. "I'm just surprised you noticed, Tucker."

He stepped closer until he was directly in front of her, towering over her, the heat of his body

24

warming her. He bent closer, placed a finger under her chin. "I always noticed."

The words should have made her melt. She'd fantasized about him saying something like that a million times. But as his lips descended toward hers, all she could feel was ...hurt. She pulled away. "It's late."

"I'm sorry, Holly. I didn't mean to do that."

But she was already down the steps, hurrying across the street, wondering if she had finally lost her mind.

Three

Mother's excitement over Tucker and the girls
coming was embarrassing.   And the fuss her
relatives made was doubly so. Did they think she
never dated? At least this year Holly hadn't once
gotten the "so when are you getting married?"
routine. If anything, she suspected her Martha-
Stewart-wannabe cousin Tiffany was mentally
planning her bridal shower.

She managed to avoid most of her relatives by
hiding in the kitchen, helping Gran with dinner.
Even though her grandmother was well into her
seventies now, she was as spry and active as
women half her age. And she was still one of
Holly's favorite people to spend time with. She and
her mother had moved here to live with Gran after
her father had left them when she was just a year
old, so she had no memories of ever having lived
elsewhere. It had always been just the three of
them, and though once in a while she had envied
those friends with "normal" lives, she had no
regrets.

"What's troubling you, Sunshine?"   Gran
asked, pulling open the oven to baste the turkey.
"You had dinner with Tucker Callahan last night;
I'd think you'd be on cloud nine today."

"I'm not fifteen anymore."

Gran gave a knowing chuckle. "Neither is he."

"What do you mean by that?"

Her grandmother finished with the baster and straightened. "Sometimes what a man can't see when he's young is crystal clear after he's had the chance to live a little."

Holly raised her brows. "I don't think I like where this conversation is heading." Especially since she had fallen back into her old habits this morning. Well, by accident. At least she hoped so. Shortly after she had gotten dressed, she heard a scraping sound from outside—the sound of someone raking leaves. There she had stood in her frilly pink and white bedroom, shelves still adorned with the dolls of her girlhood, from Holly Hobbie to Shirley Temple to Barbie, peering through the slats of her window blind. At Tucker. Outside raking leaves. But what actually held her rapt this time was not simply him, it was the joy on the faces of the two little girls diving into the piles of leaves he raked up, and his good-natured scolding when he had to re-rake them.

It was a perfect family picture, the kind she'd long ago stopped dreaming of for herself. "The only thing missing was the mommy."

"What's that dear?"

Oh God, had she said that aloud? "I think I'll set the table."

"Your mother already did."

"Oh."

Gran reached for a bottle of cooking sherry

and sprinkled some into the pan of gravy simmering on the stovetop. "Holland, what on earth is the matter with you today? You're as jumpy as a long-tailed cat—"

"In a room full of rocking chairs. I know." The doorbell chimed and, as if to prove a point, she nearly jumped out of her skin. "That will be Tucker."

"I expect so."

She heard her mother walking toward the door, heard it open. Felt the blast of cold air come down the hallway as Tucker's heavy footsteps sounded inside, heard his deep voice bellow a happy Thanksgiving. And tried to squelch a sudden urge to hide.

"Holland," Gran whispered, "aren't you going to say hello?"

She stepped across the room, picked up the cooking sherry and took a hearty drag. "Yep, I guess I will." She wiped the back of a hand across her mouth, straightened her skirt and started forward.

"The sherry?"

"What?" Halfway to the dining room, she stopped in her tracks, realizing she still clutched the bottle like a wino about to go on an all-night bender. She backed up a step and handed it off to her grandmother.

She had just reemerged from the kitchen when Tucker rounded the corner.

"There you are." He leaned in to place a kiss to her forehead just as a little hiccough escaped her.

He frowned. "Is that sherry on your breath?"

"Uh…"

He grinned down at her. The smell of him, all masculine and soapy clean, enveloped her. The sight of his off-white sweater swam before her eyes, his broad chest clouding her vision of anything else.

"How about a nice cold beer, Tucker?"

Before he could answer, her mother was there, pressing a dark green bottle into his hand.

"Since when do we keep beer in the house?" Holly asked.

"I always keep it on hand for when Tucker stops by."

"Really." Holly pinned him with a gaze. "And do you stop by to visit with my mother often?"

He gave a half smile before tipping the bottle up.

"Tucker mowed the grass for us all summer. Raked our leaves last week, too. And I would have never gotten out of the driveway during that blizzard last spring—"

"I get it, Mother." The need to disappear beneath the rug was nearly overwhelming at that point. Any minute, Mother would pull out her baby pictures and start showing those to him. If she hadn't already.

"Anyway, I like to keep some on hand for him. And apple juice for the little ones—there they are!"

Her mother crouched low, arms outstretched as the two girls rushed toward her. Oh God, it was official. Marian McCall had finally given up on grandchildren of her own and adopted someone else's. She'd even found herself a make shift son-in-law.

"Just being neighborly." Tucker met her gaze over the top of her mother's head. "It's nothing really."

Another delighted squeal emerged from the kitchen as Aspen and Sierra found Gran and were given hugs and cookies.

"How often do you stop by?" she asked.

"Oh, you know, I might say hello if I see your mother or grandmother out on the porch."

"And what do you talk about?"

He gave her elbow a playful squeeze. "You, of course."

She was prevented from further grilling when the heavily pregnant Tiffany waddled into the room. Apparently no female in her family could resist throwing themselves at him.

"Tucker Callahan," her cousin greeted. "You were a couple of years ahead of me in school, but I remember you."

"Little Tiffany McGarrity, look at you."

"Oh, this is baby number four for us," she gushed. "Due in January."

"How's your back feeling? I remember when my ex was eight months along with our youngest, she could hardly..."

Holly rolled her eyes and tuned them out, glancing into the kitchen at the sight of the two little girls seated at the counter sipping apple cider and eating cookies while Gran asked them about school. Something squeezed at her heart, a memory perhaps, of similar times with her grandmother. Or maybe it was the familiar pang of recognizing what she would never have for herself. She noticed her cousin waddling off, a hand pressed to her back.

"Listen, Holly," Tucker's breath brushed her ear. "I was hoping we could talk later."

"About what?" She turned, and too late realized he'd moved in close. Her shoulder brushed his chest, her breasts his upper arm. A spark of awareness flared through her.

"I messed up last night."

"Don't worry about it." She started to brush past him, but he caught her arm.

"More than that. I'd just... really like to talk with you."

The sight of her aunt heading toward the kitchen to help Gran set food on the table gave Holly the excuse she needed to put distance between them. "I need to help set the table."

"I'll help you."

"No. The game is on in the living room, why don't you have a seat and relax?" Without waiting for an answer, she left him there.

****

Dinner was as awkward as she had feared it might be. Well, for her at least. The two little girls, whom she had learned weren't twins but only a year apart, were well behaved. Sierra, the oldest, was outgoing and sociable; Aspen was shy and withdrawn. Holly watched them, recalling how much she had hated this holiday when she was their age, being forced to sit quietly and eat "yucky" food, but they did well. Meanwhile, her cousin's three boys tore around the room like cyclones.

"My brothers and I were like that," Tucker commented, grinning when one of the boys zoomed past, pretending to be an airplane. "I don't think we ever sat still until we were twelve."

"Not even then," Gran commented with a laugh. "I used to sit behind your family in church, remember?"

He chuckled good-naturedly.

"Boys are just different," Tiffany remarked, placing a hand to her swollen belly. "Mark and I are really looking forward to this one being a girl."

Holly forced a polite smile and poked at the food on her plate. She wasn't hungry, wasn't used to eating this much. Having Tucker seated right beside her didn't help either. As always, they were packed in tight around the table, and every time she moved, her elbow brushed his arm, or her thigh bumped his.

At last she set her fork aside and admitted defeat.

"Is that all you're going to eat?" he whispered.

She nodded.

"Even on Thanksgiving you can't give yourself permission to enjoy it?"

"I guess not."

He picked up the fork and scooped up some green bean casserole. "Open up."

She was tempted to refuse, but everyone at the table had gone still, watching them with an undisguised "isn't that cute" expression. Obediently, she opened her mouth.

"Very good. Now chew."

She obeyed, and he grinned. "See how easy that is?"

Her mother tut-tutted. "She's so self conscious about her weight."

Holly wished she could disappear under the table right then and there.

"She has to look good for television," Gran defended. "But she could at least eat for Thanksgiving."

"I eat plenty." She turned to look at Tucker and was met with another forkful of beans.

"I'm so glad we invited you over for dinner, Tucker," Gran said. "It's good to see her eating."

Holly dabbed at her lips with her napkin and reached for her water glass. "You invited him?" Surely Gran didn't mean it the way it sounded.

"Last weekend after he raked our leaves." She turned to the others at the table. "He does so much for Marian and I, and when we heard they were going to be alone for Thanksgiving, we asked him to come to dinner." She finished with a beaming smile. "We're so glad he and the girls could be with us today."

"Yes. It was downright neighborly of you, Gran." Holly slid him a glance from the corner of her eye, but he was engrossed in helping Aspen cut up her turkey.

"And some for Dora," the little girl said, pointing to her doll.

"Honey, I don't think Dora the Explorer can really eat."

"Yes, she can!"

"All right," he said patiently. "I'll cut up some for Dora."

"Okay. But she doesn't like stuffing."

Holly was almost tempted to smile at the child-like assurance. She met Tucker's blue green gaze. As it had been doing all day, her stomach twisted at the contact and the sheepish grin that came over him told her he knew he had some explaining to do.

She managed to get through dinner and desert, even managed to eat enough to satisfy her grandmother and Tucker. She helped her mother clear the table and was about to help with the dishes when her aunt took up a towel and moved to the sink. "I'll get these. You go be with your beau."

"He's not my—"

"Holly," her mother spoke up. "I've been telling the girls about your doll collection. Why don't you show them?"

She turned to see Aspen standing there, Dora clutched to her little chest and knelt to her level. "I'll bet you've never seen a Baby Chrissy doll."

The child shook her head. "This is Dora."

"She's very pretty," Holly said. "Maybe she'd like to meet some of my old friends. Would your sister like to come?"

"Daddy says she's a tomboy."

Holly laughed. "I kind of got that impression myself. But why don't we ask her anyway?"

A few minutes later, they had climbed the stairs to her old room. Aspen's eyes immediately lit on the toddler-sized doll with long brown hair and pudgy legs sitting on Holly's bed.

"This is Chrissy," Holly said, picking up the vinyl doll and handing it to the little girl.

"Can I hold her?" Aspen asked shyly.

"Sure." Holly handed over the doll, demonstrating how to make Chrissy's hair grow long or short with the pull string on her back.

"Wow," Sierra exclaimed. "Can I try?"

Aspen clutched the toy closer. "No."

"Here, let's see what we can find for you to play with." She reached for a little blonde doll dressed in blue and orange. "This is Apricot. She's a friend of Strawberry Shortcake."

The girl's face lit up. "I know that show."

"If you squeeze her tummy, she gives you apricot-scented kisses." She watched Sierra squeeze the doll and sniff, then laughed at the look of delight on her face.

Aspen was busy undressing Chrissy and turning her over. "Where do her batteries go?"

A deep laugh came from the doorway. "Not every toy has batteries."

Holly looked up to find Tucker leaning in the doorway, one thumb hooked in his belt loop.

She laughed. "Not back then they didn't."

The little one cuddled the doll close. Holly

picked up Dora the Explorer, left lying on her bed. "So tell me about Dora."

"She's sad," Aspen said, combing Chrissy's hair. "Cause she doesn't have a mommy anymore."

"Where did her mommy go?" Holly asked. It was none of her business where Kim Callahan had gone, or why Tucker seemed to have sole custody, but the child seemed so firm in her conviction.

"She died."

"Aspen," Tucker warned.

"That's very sad," Holly said in a gentle voice. "Maybe what Dora needs right now is a friend. How would she like it if Chrissy came over to stay for the weekend?" She glanced over her shoulder at Sierra. "Apricot, too."

She saw a wealth of emotion flicker through Tucker's eyes. "You have no idea what they'll do to that doll—"

Holly shrugged. "Chrissy has already survived one little girl." She looked back to Aspen. "She likes bubble baths and peanut butter toast."

"She can take *baths*?"

"Sure she can. That's the fun of not having any batteries."

"Dora can't get wet," she said, shaking her head. "She's cloth. But Daddy had to wash her once when I frow'd up on her."

"She still stinks, too," Sierra grumbled.

"Can I show her to Missus McCall?"

Holly had to swallow past a sudden lump of emotion in her throat. "I think she'd be very happy to see Chrissy played with again."

36

With a smile, Aspen carried her new friend out of the room. Sierra and Apricot followed. Holly took up the forgotten Dora, wondering at how different it looked from the toys of her youth. And Sierra was right, it did smell.

"That was really nice of you."

She glanced up at Tucker in the doorway. "I don't mind lending her the doll." She wanted to say Chrissy would enjoy it but knew he'd never understand. Not unless he'd ever had a favorite doll.

"I meant not asking her about Dora's dead mommy."

"I only pry into people's business when I have to." She set the doll aside and glanced up as he strolled into the room. "For work."

"Sometimes it's Dora's mommy who is dead, other times it's Aspen's. The doctor thinks it's easier for her to pretend her mommy died than to accept that ...well, Kim has basically abandoned them."

A familiar pain stabbed at her as she thought of her father's abandonment.

Tucker ran a hand through his hair. "I mean she still sends presents and calls, but she's wrapped up in her life in New York and her rich husband."

"I'm sorry, Tucker."

"Don't be. I have no regrets. I have two beautiful little girls, and I'm doing what I always wanted to do with my life."

"You mean the Christmas tree farm?

"No. I mean I'm making a difference in this town. Instead of selling off the land and moving away, I'm holding my ground."

She rose from the bed and walked across the room. "You really believe there's something worth saving in Castleford?" Out of habit, and maybe just for something to do, she bent and peered through the blinds at the dark night.

"I'm not out there."

Straightening, she turned to face him. "What is that supposed to mean?"

"Isn't this the window you used to watch me from? Like you were this morning."

"I was... watching the girls play."

He chuckled. "I don't mind, you know. I never did."

She returned to the bed and picked up the well-loved, smelly, plush doll Aspen had left behind. "I'm sure you didn't."

His hands settled on her shoulders, warm, reassuring. He turned her to face him. "I'm right here, Hol. And I've been dying to kiss you all afternoon."

He didn't give her a chance to resist. He bent his head, his lips brushing hers, soft at first, and oh so gentle. For a split second the memory of their first and last kiss taunted her, and for a moment she was that pudgy-seventeen-year-old again, heart soaring with the thrill of Tucker Callahan finally noticing her. But she pushed all thoughts of the heartache that always followed aside. She was a woman now.

The Dora doll still in one hand, she wrapped her arms about his neck and poured herself into his kiss, opening her mouth, urging him to deepen it.

He didn't disappoint. He groaned and pulled her in closer, his thighs brushing hers, his hands moving to her waist.

The floor tilted beneath her and her head spun as if she'd had too much wine. He tasted of coffee and pumpkin pie. The smell of outdoors and the crisp fall air clung to his hair and his sweater as if it were a part of him. Her fingers sought and found the hair at the nape of his neck and curled into it.

No kiss had ever rocked her senses so, and no man had ever kissed her the way Tucker did. This topped every memory she had about their first encounter, two awkward teenagers giving in to attraction and curiosity. This was so much better, so much sweeter.

His hands moved up her waist, thumbs brushing the sides of her breasts. Oh God, she wanted him to touch her, wanted to feel his hands on her body. Against her stomach, she felt the hard length of him behind his zipper and knew he wanted the same thing she did.

At last he broke the kiss. She slid her hands down his chest, marveled at the solid feel of him beneath the sweater. But she didn't move out of his arms, couldn't bring herself to leave the warmth and security she found there. "Why didn't you tell me you had already been invited to dinner?"

He laughed deeply. "Sorry about that. I knew your mother and grandmother only wanted to fix us up. I had to be sure you were interested, too."

The words were like a cold shower washing over her. Fixed up? She couldn't possibly begin a relationship now. Their lives were heading in different directions.

She took a step backward. The cozy feeling she'd enjoyed in his embrace abruptly vanished, and she rubbed her arms against a sudden chill.

"I said the wrong thing again, didn't I?"

"No, I should have realized they were—"

"Holly?" came Tiffany's voice from the bottom of the stairs. "We're just getting ready to leave."

Holly edged toward the door. "We'd better get down there before they get suspicious."

"You're right. Two single, attractive adults like us. How would that look?"

"Tucker, I'm sorr—"

"For what?"

"I can't get involved with anyone right now. I just can't." She handed him the doll and hurried from the room. She should be angry at Gran and Mom for trying to fix her up but she couldn't blame them. They just didn't understand that not everyone's happiness came from marriage and family. Hers came from her career.

The last thing she needed was Tucker Callahan with his blue-green eyes and earth-tilting kisses making her second guess herself.

Four

The girls were tucked in sound asleep—all four of them. Sierra, Aspen, Dora and Chrissy. When he'd checked on his youngest a short time ago, Tucker had found her clutching both dolls.

He wandered aimlessly through the house. When he and his brothers had been growing up, at times the old house had seemed small. But on nights like this, it was enormous. Empty and cold, like it was just waiting for a family to fill it with life and laughter again.

But his restlessness was due to more than loneliness. Odd, but he missed Holly. And the way she kissed him, she sure as hell must be feeling the same thing. He'd never been the spontaneous type and sex with Kim—when she'd allowed it—had never exactly been mind-bending. But this afternoon he could have easily made love to Holly right there on that doll-strewn bed. He'd been that turned on. And it wasn't just because she was strikingly beautiful. It was everything. The way she really seemed to listen when he talked; the gentle way she was with the girls; the dry sense of humor he remembered from their school days together.

I can't get involved with anyone right now. I

41

just can't.

The words had been echoing in his brain half the night. Why? She said she wasn't seeing anyone, and with an attraction like theirs, they'd be fools not to at least give it a try. Sure she lived and worked five hours away, but he was willing to give it a shot.

He opened the front door and stepped onto the porch. The cold night air was tinged with the smell of wood smoke, but the sky was clear and the stars bright. He glanced at the old porch swing, swaying slightly. An idea struck him.

An hour and a half later, he stood out in the middle of the street, wondering if he was as much a fool as he felt at that moment. He had to try. Had to convince Holly this connection they felt was worth it—that *he* was worth it.

He scooped up a handful of stones and began to pelt them one at a time toward her window. The first two missed and struck the house, but the third, fourth and fifth hit their mark. A dim light went on inside the room, and then the window slid open.

Holly poked her head out. "What are you doing?"

"Trying to wake you."

"I wasn't asleep."

"Having trouble sleeping?" He hoped to God it was because of him, but wasn't brave enough to ask.

"Well, it is a little difficult when someone's throwing rocks at my window."

42

"I'll stop if you come down."

She turned to look at something behind her. "Do you realize it's nearly midnight?"

"So?"

"Don't you have to work in the morning?"

"Come on, Hol'. Come down and talk to me."

"Go to bed, Tucker." She slid the window closed.

He was about to turn and admit defeat. Tomorrow would start the busiest season of the year for him; he should take her advice and go to bed. But instead of heading across the street he pulled in a deep breath, and as loud as he could, began to sing. *"Oh, you'd better watch out, better not cry, better not pout, I'm telling you why..."*

The window opened again. "Tucker Callahan, are you drunk?"

"Not in the least. But I'm going to stand out here and sing until I either wake the whole town or you come down here." He drew in another breath. *"Santa Claus is comin' to town..."*

"Shh!" She put a finger to her lips. "All right, I'll come. But this had better be important."

A few seconds later the porch light came on. Holly stepped out, dressed in an oversized pink sweatshirt, pink and blue checked pants and fuzzy pink slippers. She placed her hands to her hips. "What?"

He stepped up onto the porch and took hold of her hand. "I want to show you something." With a tug, he led her across the street and onto his porch. It was too dark for her to see the tray with the thermos of hot cocoa he'd made or the heavy blanket he'd brought out, but he signaled for her to wait while he reached inside the door and flicked the light switch on.

The porch was immediately bathed in a soft, multicolored glow of Christmas lights. In the yard, two brightly-lit gingerbread people stood guard over a gingerbread house while Santa waved from a sleigh with animated reindeer and glowing presents within. An inflatable snow globe containing Snoopy and the Peanuts gang was off to one side of the yard; a complete life-size nativity scene sat beneath an evergreen tree.

She looked around, her face brightening in appreciation. "When did you find the time to do this?"

"Just now."

She fixed him with another of those reporter-sharp gazes. "Okay, I get it. You're not drunk, you're insane."

"Maybe a little." He laughed and grabbed hold of her hand before she could retreat. "Come sit with me."

"It's freezing out here."

"I promise to keep you warm." He stepped to the porch swing and shook out the blanket. "Come on."

Indecision crossed her face. "Tucker..."

"I know you can't get involved with anyone." He shrugged. "I'm not asking you to be. I'm simply asking my neighbor to sit on my front porch with me." He wanted to ask for more than that. A lot more. But she was as skittish as a wild rabbit. He held up the thermos for her to see. "Hot chocolate. Extra marshmallows."

She raised an eyebrow. "It's not the kind you make with hot water, is it?"

"Noooo," he lied. "Made it myself just moments ago."

"You're a terrible liar, Tucker Callahan. But since it's barely thirty degrees out here, I'll take you up on that watery cocoa." She took a seat on the swing, and for a moment he hesitated. How close should he sit? Maybe he should let her get a little chilly first, and then she would slide closer. Then again, maybe he should stop over-thinking everything.

He sat. Near enough that she could scoot closer if she wanted, but not so far that he couldn't feel the warmth of her beside him. He reached for the thermos and mugs he had brought out earlier.

"*Two* mugs?" Holly said knowingly. "Were you expecting company?"

"I was," he admitted, pouring one for her. "You."

He filled his own mug, set the thermos aside and stretched an arm along the back of the swing. To his great relief she shifted closer, murmuring something about how cold it was. "Sky's clear tonight," he said, searching for conversation.

"A winter sky," she murmured, tipping back to look. The movement brought her head into contact with his shoulder, and he closed his eyes to savor the sensation. She didn't move away. He curled his arm closer, fingers stroking her silky hair.

"You know, I didn't really spend my entire girlhood watching you out the window."

"Of course not," he said, letting his tone tell her he didn't believe her.

She laughed and gently nudged his ribs with her elbow. "I didn't."

"I liked that you did." His voice came out strangled as he recalled those years. "You looking up at me with those adoring brown eyes was something I could always depend on. Like the change of the seasons."

"Was I that transparent?"

"Sometimes." He winced at the memory of his friends ribbing him about Fat Holly. How foolish it seemed now, but at the time it had really bothered him how they picked on her. They had made fun of her for her weight, which looking back on it wasn't all that much, and her clothes, which were never in fashion. But then she was smarter than all of them. And they'd known it.

When she drew her knees up, he tucked the blanket around her. "I hated football season, you know." She adjusted the blanket and looked up at him with those deep, doe-brown eyes. "You had practice after school every day."

He tugged her hair with a gentle pull. "We couldn't walk home from school together."

"Exactly. When it wasn't football season, I used to hurry out of my last class so I could 'accidentally' meet up with you as you were leaving."

"I figured that," he gave a soft chuckle. "Sometimes I'd hang around and wait for you."

"You did?"

"Like I said before, Holly; I always noticed you."

"Then why—" Her voice broke; she glanced down at the cup in her hand. "I was too pathetic for you to ever consider dating me."

"Never pathetic, Holly. Not to me anyway. But I was seventeen and seventeen-year-old guys are jerks."

"Tell me about it."

"Do you date the un-cool girl your friends will tease you about? Or do you date the cheerleader you're expected to?"

"You kissed me."

So she did remember. In her grandmother's kitchen. Senior year. The night they had finished Mister Moore's science project. "Yes."

"Then the next day you were in the hall between classes kissing Melissa Logan."

He swallowed hard. So she remembered that, too. "I didn't want to hurt you."

A choking sound escaped her. On impulse, he grabbed hold of her arm before she could flee. "Don't go." He pulled her against him, breast to chest. "It was thirteen years ago, Hol. Forgive me for being an idiot. I thought if you saw me kissing other girls it would be easier for you to accept that kissing you didn't mean anything that night."

"It did to me." The glow of the Christmas lights above glinted in her hair, changing it from pink to green to blue as the colors changed. But the dark eyes staring up at him glistened with anguish.

"You never said anything. You never spoke to me again."

"Why would I?" She began to rise, but he held tight.

"Don't punish me for being a stupid kid back then."

"Because I've lost weight, and I look different now, it's okay to be seen with me? I won't ruin your image this way?"

Sliding his hold from her arm to her hand, he rose. "Is that what you think?"

"It's the truth, isn't it?" She rose to face him. "For eighteen years we were neighbors, and you never threw rocks at my window or put up Christmas lights and invited me to sit on your front porch."

"Aw, Holly." He reached to pull her into his arms, but she dodged away. "The only difference I see now is you're finally as beautiful on the outside as you always were on the inside."

A sob escaped her, and she turned away from him. He heard her draw in a sniffle, saw her shoulders tremble. "How long did it take you to come up with that line?"

"About a minute." Still unwilling to let her go and leave things like this, he moved a hand to her shoulder. "I don't want to screw up again, Holly."

Another sniffle. He groped for the right words to convince her it wasn't her looks he was interested in this time around. "You know when your mother and grandmother brag about your accomplishments, they don't talk about things like losing weight or dying your hair. They talk about *you*. How talented you are, how driven." He spun her around to face him and couldn't help a smile at the tear-streaked face and red nose. *"That's* the Holly I've been wanting to see again."

"Oh, Tucker." She went up on tiptoe to wrap her arms about his neck. Her soft breasts were crushed against his chest, the sweet, flowery scent of her perfume teased his nose. Awareness rocketed through him. She turned her head, her lips achingly close to his. "You kissed me tonight," she murmured. "Who will I find you kissing tomorrow?"

"You." To prove his point, he took her mouth, kissing her tenderly. Her lips parted beneath his and with the first taste, warm and tinged with hot cocoa, he was lost. Head spinning, knee-trembling lost.

She shivered, and while he liked to think it was because of him, he was freezing his ass off. He led her back toward the swing, sat down and pulled her in close beside him, tucking the blanket around them.

"Do you want more cocoa?" he asked, reaching for the thermos.

"No." She put a hand to his arm. "Just more of you."

"I think I can manage that." He grinned and bent to kiss her again. His hands moved to her waist, sliding over her hips. Her sweatshirt rode up a bit, and he felt the heat of her satiny skin beneath his palm, heard her breath catch as he boldly explored, hands smoothing up her back. Either he was too weak to resist temptation or his hands had a mind of their own, because before he could even think about it, one stole around to stroke her breast. She sighed and then moaned as he filled his palm with soft flesh. He molded her breast, thumb stealing across her nipple. Unable to stop himself, he slid his other hand beneath the sweatshirt and found and caressed the other as well.

"Holly," He couldn't move, couldn't think, could do nothing but feel. And want.

Her hands moved over his shoulders and chest, sliding over his arms and back up. Soft moans of pleasure escaped her, emboldening him to continue. He wanted to touch her everywhere and all at once. More than anything, he wanted to taste her.

He glanced at his hands on her breasts; small and firm, they fit his palms perfectly. He bent to swirl his tongue around one rosy nipple. She groaned aloud, fingers sliding into his hair while he stroked and teased and suckled first one breast and then the other.

"Tucker? What if someone walks by?"

He'd been wondering the same thing himself. "You know they roll up the sidewalks around here at six p.m. No one will." Nonetheless, he rose and took hold of her hand. "Do you want to come inside?"

Her gaze, sleepy with desire, met his. She nodded.

He wanted to whoop with delight, carry her inside and throw her on the couch, but she'd probably find the Neanderthal approach a turn-off. Instead, he steeled himself to move slowly, held open the door and let her in.

She turned to him as he closed the front door with a gentle click. She took hold of his hand and led him into the darkened living room, pulling him down on the couch with her. He resumed kissing her, pulling her onto his lap so that she straddled him. His hands stole beneath her sweatshirt again, making no pretense this time, but heading straight for her breasts. She tugged the shirt off and arched closer. One breast found its way to his mouth, while his hand caressed the other. His free hand slid over her hips, slipping beneath the waistband of her flannel pants to slide over one soft buttock. She moved against him, finding his throbbing erection through his jeans and sliding over it. He shifted, thrusting against her.

"Tucker," she whispered against his mouth, "tell me you have a condom."

Cold realization washed over him. He'd forgotten about that. And since he wasn't actively dating, he'd never thought to keep them on hand. He tore his mouth from her breast. "Uh oh."

She laughed. "And in this town there's no such thing as a twenty-four-hour store."

"Not until that new super Walmart opens up."

He sighed and raked a hand through his hair.

"I thought all single guys kept them around, just in case."

"Not single guys with nosy daughters."

"We were probably rushing a little too much anyway."

He sure as hell hadn't thought so. In fact, it felt completely right. But before he could answer, he heard the patter of little feet overhead a moment before the plaintive *"Daaa-adddy?"* at the top of the stairs.

Holly moved off him so fast he was surprised she didn't trip.

A cough and a sniffle came before he could get to his feet.

The soft thump of Sierra's slippers coming down the stairs followed.

"Hey, baby girl," he said, scooping her up at the bottom of the stairs. "What are you doing awake?"

She lay a sleepy head on his shoulder and sniffled. "I can't sleep."

Holly had retreated to the shadows, apparently not wanting to be seen. He met her gaze as he carried Sierra into the kitchen. This was an almost nightly ritual, her waking and coming to find him. It had been since the divorce. A little chocolate milk, a bit of cuddling and she'd be all set.

He had just rounded the corner to the kitchen when Sierra lifted her head. "Why is Holly here?"

"She, uh...helped me put up some Christmas

lights outside for you and your sister. It was supposed to be a surprise." He tapped the end of her nose playfully. "But now it won't be."

She smiled and snuggled back into his shoulder while he carried her to the kitchen table and set her down.

Holly appeared in the doorway, looking as awkward as he felt. "I should... probably..." She pointed over her shoulder toward the front door.

It wasn't the way he wanted to end things tonight. But he couldn't very well ask her to stay. It was late, and who knew how long it would be until Sierra settled down again. "Will I see you tomorrow?"

"Oh, I don't know. Maybe."

He wasn't about to let her get away that easy. Tempted as he was to invite her to stop by the farm tomorrow, he'd be busy and unable to spend time with her. "I'm taking the girls to have their pictures done tomorrow afternoon. Come with me."

"Oh, I couldn't intrude—"

"Can Holly do our hair?" Sierra piped up. "I want mine to be pretty like hers."

And to think he hadn't even had to bribe the kid to get her to say that. He gave Holly what he hoped was a helpless look. "I can only do ponytails. Curls or ribbons and I'm all thumbs."

"I'll do their hair."

"And have dinner with us afterward," he insisted.

"Please?" Sierra sing-songed

"A–allright," she finally relented, looking a

53

little like a trapped deer.

Tucker squelched the satisfied grin he felt rising.

"Okay, pumpkin, you sit tight. I'm going to walk Holly across the street, and I'll be right back."

Sierra slid off the table, cup of chocolate milk in hand, and followed him to the front door, oohing and ahhing over the twinkling lights.

Not only would he have dinner with Holly tomorrow night, but he'd stop by the drugstore on his way to work in the morning and assure them a pleasant night afterward.

Five

While Christmas music poured from overhead speakers, Holly stared blearily at the half-empty coffee mug before her. She'd barely slept, but had promised Mom and Gran they'd go out to breakfast and then spend the day shopping. After years of working one of her two jobs, the now-retired Marian was ready enjoy the day after Thanksgiving.

And Holly was determined to give her a day of shopping with her daughter, if that's what she wanted. No matter how tired and distracted she was.

In fact, in the few hours since leaving Tucker's house, he had hardly been away from her thoughts. She'd lain in her bed and tossed and turned, the memory of his touch and the fierce need it had awakened, preventing any chance of rest. Just as the sun had begun to rise, she'd heard his truck start across the street. She rolled onto her stomach and peeked through the blinds, watching the red glow of his taillights as he brushed a light dusting of snow off the truck, then piled the two girls into the back seat and buckled them in.

Despite better judgment, she'd found herself wondering who watched the girls while he worked, and if he was as tired this morning as she. Wondering about all the minute details of his daily life. And for once she hadn't felt the cold empty sense of not belonging. She'd felt a warm rush to know, that in some small way, she was a part of his world.

Oh God, she was pathetic.

Marge the waitress, complete with beehive hairdo, pencil tucked over her ear, bright red lipstick and snapping gum approached the table. "Mornin' hon," she said, greeting Marian. "Sure ain't the same workin' here without you."

Holly watched as her mother flushed. "Feels strange not to be here. But I like it."

The two women shared a giggle as Marge handed menus around. "Well, you're missin' all the good gossip."

"What did I miss?" Marian straightened in her seat. "Who is it about?"

The waitress glanced dramatically over each shoulder before speaking. "Floyd the pharmacist was just in here. Said he had a customer bright and early this morning." She reached over to refill their coffee mugs.

"Heavens," Gran said. "I hope no one is sick."

"Oh, they ain't sick," Marge cackled. "You'll never guess what this person was buying at seven o'clock this morning."

Holly felt a tingle of warning move across her skin and resisted the urge to slide beneath the table.

Marge leaned in with a conspiratorial whisper.

"*Safes.*"

Marian gasped and put a hand over her mouth. Holly had to search her foggy, sleep-deprived brain for a moment before remembering that was what her mother's generation called condoms.

"Who was it?

Marge did another dramatic check behind her before grinning and mouthing the words, "Tucker Callahan."

To their credit, both her mother and grandmother looked surprised. Or had they not heard his Christmas serenade last night?

"Tucker's been back in town for months now; I didn't know he was seeing anyone." Gran said, flashing a curious glance at Holly. "We just saw him yesterday, and he never mentioned it."

Just like everyone else in this town, they couldn't wrap their minds around the idea of Tucker and Fat Holly.

Marge put a hand to her hip. "Well, I know the widda Tompkins watches his girls while he's working."

"Oh," Marian scoffed. "Arlynn Tompkins is sixty if she's a day."

"Maybe it's some divorcee outside of town," Gran offered with a nod. Holly bit the inside of her cheek to keep from smiling at that. In Gran's mind any scandal had to involve a "divorcee."

"Who in the devil could it be?" Marge stared off into space thoughtfully, gum snapping. "Floyd said that boy looked like he hadn't had a lick of sleep all night."

Gran set her coffee cup down with a thunk, and the gazes of all three women came to rest on Holly.

Flushing, she slumped lower in her seat. She'd put makeup on the dark circles beneath her eyes this morning, but it didn't hide the puffiness. Clearing her throat, she held up a menu. "Could I just have the breakfast special, please?"

****

The mall where the girls had their pictures done was nearly an hour's drive away, something Holly supposed the people of Castleford were used to by now. But she had grown accustomed to living closer to malls and restaurants. Now, on the way back, the country roads were dark and snow-covered.

The excited chatter from the two little girls in the back seat had ceased a while ago; she suspected they had fallen asleep. Staring at the dark hills and countryside awash in white, Holly marveled at how the sight could still move her.

There was something about a fresh coating of snow that made everything feel pristine again, like a clean slate or a new beginning. Somehow, tonight, it seemed as magical to see the snow coming down as it had when she was a little girl.

And everything about this moment was so right, so perfect.

A stab of longing pierced her heart. Why did this have to happen now? Things were just starting to take off in her professional life. Why did Tucker and those sweet little girls have to come along now?

"You're quiet," he said, his thumb brushing over the hand that rested on her thigh. She closed her eyes as skitters of awareness moved through her. Every look, every innocent touch all evening had affected her this way.

She smiled at him despite the heaviness that settled over her heart.

"Do you want the radio on?"

"No, it's fine." And it really was. Even the silence was comfortable, crackling with sexual attraction, but... *comfortable*. She didn't feel the need to grope for conversation. Instead, it felt as though they'd done this a million times.

He glanced in the mirror, and a soft smile lifted the corners of his mouth. "They're asleep."

She turned to look over her shoulder and her heart melted. Sierra, who had her father's charm, and sweet Aspen, so vulnerable and fragile that she reminded Holly of herself at that age. When had she fallen in love with them? *All* of them?

Tucker cleared his throat. "Uh, Holly...I need to tell you something."

She brought her attention back to him. "This sounds serious."

"No, but uh..." He cleared his throat again. "I'd forgotten how fast talk can travel in a town this size."

A flush of warmth stole over her cheeks. "Tucker—"

He stared straight ahead, unwilling to meet

59

her gaze. "It's stupid, but I stopped into the drugstore this morning, and now—"

"I know."

"You do?"

"I heard about it at breakfast this morning. The whole town knows."

He grimaced, shook his head. "My brothers spent the day riding me about it, and everyone who stopped to buy a wreath or a tree today—wait a minute, how did you hear about it?"

"Floyd comes into the diner for his coffee. He told Marge."

"And if Marge knows..." He released a loud breath.

"Everyone knows."

"Well, that's great," he wiped a hand down his face. "I'm sorry, Holly. I know you must be embarrassed."

"Actually, I think it's kind of funny."

"I thought you'd be mad." He reached across to take her hand again. "I don't want you to think I...expect anything."

"Maybe *I* expect it." She couldn't believe she'd said it. But she had to leave Sunday morning, and wasn't sure when she'd be back. More than anything she wanted to take the memory of making love to Tucker with her when she left.

****

Tucker leaned in the doorway of Aspen's purple and white "Princess" bedroom and listened to the story coming from within.

"And then Princess Dora—"

"And Cwissy."

"*And* her friend Princess Chrissy, lived in the castle happily ever after."

Something twisted his gut into knots at the sound of Holly's gentle voice. He'd tucked Sierra in, she'd barely even woke when he'd put her pajamas on, but Aspen had wakened when they got back to the house and insisted Holly help tuck her in. He worried about his youngest getting so attached so soon. But then, he had, too.

He wasn't an impulsive man. Had never considered falling in love in the space of a weekend. But he had. Or maybe he'd been half in love with Holly McCall his entire life and she'd finally managed to push him over the edge. Either way, he was there. Or at least well on his way.

"Tell it again," Aspen insisted.

"Not now." Holly's tone was gentle. "It's very late. Maybe tomorrow night."

"Will you be here tomorrow night at bedtime, Holly?"

"We'll see." She reached for the lamp at Aspen's bedside and switched it off.

"Sing me a song."

"Go to sleep, Aspen," he said, stepping into the room.

She smiled up at him from beneath her Princess bedspread. "Okay."

Holly moved past him toward the doorway, and he caught the smell of her perfume. The tug of attraction hit him hard.

"Holly?" came a small voice from within the

61

darkened room. "You aren't gonna leave, too, are you?"

"I have to go back to Syracuse Sunday morning, Aspen."

"When will you come back?"

Tucker held his breath, wanting to ask her the same thing, even though he assumed she'd be home for Christmas. But he couldn't let Aspen put her on the spot like that, couldn't allow his daughter to make plans. Not just yet.

"I'm sure Holly will come visit us next time she's home," he said. "Now go to sleep or I'm going to have to e-mail Santa and tell him all the naughty things you've been up to."

His daughter's mouth opened in an exaggerated O of surprise before she pulled the blankets over her head. He grinned. He hadn't seen her this light-hearted and playful in a long time.

Downstairs, he pulled the half empty bottle of wine from the other night from the fridge and filled two glasses. He felt Holly come up behind him and turned.

"There's something I've been wanting to do all day," he said, and without giving her a chance to answer, pulled her in for a kiss. He'd intended it only as a quick kiss to satisfy the need to taste her, feel her close to him again. But after a day of being away from her and an evening of being tortured by her nearness, it turned into more. Their mouths melted together, tasting, touching, drinking the other in. Her hands smoothed up his back in a slow caress that molded him to her, the softness of her breasts crushing against him.

When she finally pulled back from the kiss, she wrapped her arms about his neck and held tight. He felt a shudder move through her.

"Is everything all right?" he asked, a little confused by the sudden turn of emotion.

"Great," she said, her voice muffled by his shoulder. "Just hold me for a minute."

He had no idea if that was the kind of "holding" that led to sex, or if it was the kind of holding *instead* of sex, but he didn't care. Just being close to her was enough right now. Besides, he couldn't shake the feeling that they had the rest of their lives ahead of them for lovemaking.

"Come with me," he said and led her into the living room. He switched on the radio that sat atop the fireplace, and Christmas music poured into the room.

Holly groaned. "I hate Holiday music."

"But it gives us an excuse to do this," he said, pulling her to him once again and beginning to sway as Nat King Cole's voice led them.

She wrapped her arms about his neck once again, inhaled deeply from the curve of his neck. "You still smell like Tucker."

He pulled back a little to look at her. "That's because I *am* Tucker."

She placed a hand to his cheek and kissed him. He felt the moisture of tears from her cheeks against his.

"Is there something going on I should know

about? Or does Nat King Cole always make you cry?"

"Nothing, there's nothing," she whispered. "I'm just happy and sad all at once."

"I can fix that," he promised against her lips. He wished he'd taken time to start a fire in the fireplace, or at least piled some comfortable pillows in front of it. But the couch would have to do.

He scooped her into his arms and carried her to the sofa. Feeling a little too warm, and because he wanted to feel the heat of her body against him, he pulled his sweater off, leaving just a dark blue tee shirt.

Holly trailed a hand over his chest and down one of his biceps. "How does a Christmas tree farmer get a body like this?"

"Hard work." He dropped a kiss to her lips. "And maybe that gym I have set up in the basement. I've had a lot of frustration to work off the past couple years."

She laughed, all signs of the tears gone. "Sexual frustration?"

"Among other things."

"Well, maybe *I* can fix *that*," she teased, sliding a hand down his stomach to his belt. "I've been wondering what's beneath these faded Levi's all night." She moved her hand lower, cupping his hard length. He couldn't help the groan that escaped him.

"Is it safe to do this here?" she whispered. "I worry about the girls interrupting…"

"I'll hear them long before they get down the

64

stairs," he assured her. Besides, he didn't want her to see the mess he'd left his bedroom in. And because he couldn't allow her to stay the night, couldn't confuse the girls that way. Right now they thought of her as a family friend, and he intended to keep it that way. But Holly's hand on his throbbing erection robbed him of all coherent thought, making it hard to breathe, let alone reason.

He fingered the hem of her black turtle neck sweater. "I've been wondering what's under this myself." Though he much preferred the easy access clothing from last night, he'd spent the evening pondering the secrets hidden beneath the soft sweater and low rise jeans.

He lifted the hem just enough to brush his fingertips over her stomach. He heard her intake of breath, saw the desire flare in her eyes as he raised the sweater. Her porcelain skin and flat, toned stomach was revealed inch by inch. Unable to resist the creamy oasis before him, he bent to press his lips to the smooth skin, dragged his tongue across it and around her naval.

Her fingers tangled in his hair, and she breathed his name, the sound breathless and completely turned on. He wanted to hear that sound again, wanted to drive her to the edge and drag her over with him.

He took his time kissing his way up her stomach toward her breasts, driven by her sighs and moans. At last he raised the sweater to reveal the black satin and velvet beneath and paused to appreciate the sight before him. "Aw, Hol," he said, brushing a hand over the soft material, fingers gliding over a taut nipple outlined against the lace. "I should have made love to you thirteen years ago."

A laugh escaped her. "In my grandmother's kitchen?"

He raised up to kiss her. "There and a few other places."

She twined her arms about his neck. "I'm glad we waited."

"I'm just sorry we wasted so much time."

Her lips met his, and he was lost in the taste and smell of her again, only aware of the feel of her—soft breasts, warm velvet and lace. The clasp between her breasts gave way on the first try. He held his breath while he slid a hand over the warmth of her skin. And then she filled his palm, her sighs filling his ears as he stroked her. He tore his mouth from hers, unable to resist the sight of his hands on her breasts, then bent, swirling his tongue around one pink nipple.

Holly threw her head back as sensation washed over her, closing her eyes to savor the moment. She'd had boyfriends over the years, but nothing had ever compared to the exquisite wonder of Tucker. And they had barely gotten started. How was it possible she was on the verge of orgasm, and he had hardly touched her? Yet at the same time, she needed more, wanted to feel his skin against hers—everywhere.

In desperation, she reached for the hem of his

tee shirt, tugging it from his waistband and yanking it up. He obliged her, easing up to shrug out of it.

"Oooh," she said, easing her hands over the broad shoulders and down his hard, muscled chest. She trailed her fingernails through the soft brown hairs sprinkled across his chest. "I'd say you've been *very* frustrated, Tucker." She continued her journey toward the waist of his jeans, and over the sizable bulge in his jeans, then unfastened them and tugged down his zipper. The full length of him sprang free, and she wrapped a hand around him.

"*Daaaa-aaady?*"

Holly jumped back, scrambling for something to cover herself with.

He rose to fasten his jeans. "It's all right, it's Aspen. She's scared to get out of bed when it's dark." He bent to drop a kiss before walking away. "I'll be right back."

"I'm not going anywhere."

He looked back over his shoulder at her and grinned.

Holly heard the stairs groan beneath his feet as he climbed them, the creaking of floorboards overhead.

She looked around the darkened living room and noticed the heavy blanket from the porch last night draped over a chair. She rose and took it up, spreading it on the floor in front of the cold fireplace. She retuned to the couch for a couple of pillows and arranged them before it, then to the kitchen for their forgotten glasses of wine. Out the kitchen window, she noticed the snow still falling steadily.

She hated snow, hated to drive in it, hated dealing with it every day during the winter—and Syracuse certainly got more than its share of storms. But there was something enchanting about the magical way it fell to the ground tonight, flakes drifting toward the ground as though someone had just shaken up a snow globe.

Back in the living room, she pulled the curtains open and looked out. Across the street, a row of stately Victorian houses were snow covered, reminding her of an old fashioned Christmas card. The branches on the big pine tree in front of Gran's house were bent low from the weight of their white caps, the lights they had hung this afternoon twinkling.

Funny how in her memories she never saw Castleford quite this way. It always seemed darker to her somehow. But now she saw it for what it was—a quaint little town from a bygone era; a slice of Americana that was gradually fading away.

For the first time she understood Tucker's desire to return and do his part to keep it thriving.

A lump rose in her throat as she soaked in the sight of Gran's old house. She'd always loved it. But her job was calling her far away; it would be a long time before she'd see it again, and probably never quite like this.

Tucker's footsteps coming down the stairs had her turning from the window to see if he was alone.

"Still snowing," he said.

"Yes, it's beautiful," she whispered. "Is Aspen all right?"

"Fine. Dora fell out of bed and she was scared to get out and get her."

She smiled. "Sweet."

He pulled her into his arms and kissed her. Again, unable to help herself, she slid her hands over his bare chest and shoulders, the fire between them flaring anew.

"Where were we?" he asked nuzzling her neck, hand slipping beneath her sweater to find and caress her breast.

"Mmmm," she moaned as he teased her nipple. "Right about there." She took hold of his hand and led him toward the fireplace.

"What's this?" he asked as they dropped to their knees together on the blankets.

"I thought it was more cozy."

He took her face between his hands. "I'm sorry there's no fire, Hol. No candles. Nothing to make it special. I'm not very good at romantic gestures."

"You're more than good at them, Tucker Callahan. And just look at the view out that window," she nodded toward the curtains. "Nothing could make tonight more special than that."

He groaned and leaned in to kiss her. "You're an incredible woman, Holly McCall."

The words burned in the back of her brain as he kissed her. His hands moved beneath her sweater to caress her again. He tugged it over her head once more, bending to kiss her breasts as they were once again bared to him. Holly arched against him as he smoothed his hands over her buttocks, molding her to him.

She slipped her hands over his shoulders and back, cupping his firm, muscular behind before moving one hand between them to unfasten his jeans.

He groaned low in his throat as she freed him once more, took him in her hand, explored the hard, satiny length. He rested his head in the curve of her neck. "Hol," he breathed against her skin. "You're killing me."

She started to pull her hand away, but he closed his fingers around her wrist.

"In a good way," he assured her, lifting his head to kiss her again. And then he eased her down onto the blanket, knuckles brushing her abdomen as he unbuttoned her jeans and tugged the zipper down. She held her breath as he swept the jeans from her legs and tossed them aside.

He murmured something unintelligible and bent to drop a kiss to her abdomen. He lay alongside her on the blanket and shoved his jeans off, pushing his boxers down at the same time. She rolled to meet him, her mouth seeking his, hands needing to touch him.

He moved over her, one hand slipping between them to stroke her intimately. She moved against his touch, wanting, needing to feel him inside her. She reached to slide off her panties and heard his low moan in response, felt the change in his breathing when he touched her. And found her ready for him.

"Oh God, Holly."

He dragged his jeans over and fumbled in the pocket for something.

"Ahh, so that's where you're hiding them," she teased when he produced the little foil packet. He tore it open, rolled it on, then positioned himself over her.

She gazed up into his face, the face of the man she had loved for so many years. She'd spent her life comparing other men to him—and they'd always come up lacking. Tears gathered in the corners of her eyes. She whispered his name, and he eased inside her. He began to move, slowly, gently, until they found a rhythm together. She wrapped her legs around his waist. He thrust hard and deep, and she cried out as a climax rocked her. She clung to him as the spasms washed over her, carrying her to even greater heights as he groaned aloud and followed her, bathing her soul in a glow as warm and vivid as the Christmas lights twinkling outside the window.

In that moment, she felt joined to him in so much more than just the physical; it was as if he had filled her completely, body and soul.

At long last, Holland McCall had found her way home.

Six

Despite being tired, Tucker had a smile on his face more often than not throughout the day. Memories of making love to Holly well into the early dawn hours kept him company. That and the stunned look on Floyd the Pharmacist's face this morning when he'd strolled back into the pharmacy at seven a.m. To buy another box of condoms.

He couldn't wait to see Holly tonight, couldn't wait to make love to her again. Sure, she'd be heading back to Syracuse tomorrow morning, and long distance relationships were a bitch, but he had a feeling they wouldn't be apart for long. One way or another, they'd find a way to be together. But it had to be Holly's choice, he'd never ask her to move back to Castleford. Fortunately, she wasn't so far away that they couldn't see each other most weekends and get used to the whole idea of becoming a family.

The sky was beginning to darken as his older brother approached his truck. "Where do you want that tree?" He thumbed over his shoulder toward a tree they had set aside earlier in the day.

Tucker pulled on his heavy work gloves. "I'll toss it in the back of the truck."

"Need some help?"

"Nah, I got it." He hoisted the tree onto a shoulder and dropped it in the bed of the pick up.

"Where was it you said you were going tonight?"

"No place special. But I appreciate you covering for me."

"No problem." His brother leaned against the truck. "You sure are in a good mood."

Grinning, he threw his gloves in the workbox in the back of the truck and moved around to the driver's side door. "Am I?"

"Is it true what I've been hearing about you and Holly McCall?"

Still grinning, he yanked open the door and faced his brother. "Depends on what you've been hearing?"

"That you're keeping Floyd in business. And that she's not Fat Holly anymore."

"She never was." He opened the door and climbed in. Warmth spread through him at the thought of the night ahead, about his plans to put a ring on a branch of the tree on Christmas Eve. He'd give her all the time she needed to answer him. But he wasn't stupid enough to lose her twice in a lifetime.

The drive home seemed shorter than usual, the songs on the radio all ones he liked to sing along with. He'd told Mrs. Tompkins he'd be a few minutes later than usual to pick up the girls, he had a tree to deliver.

He stepped onto the front porch, whistling a Christmas carol and rang the bell. Moments later

Holly answered.

"Merry Christmas," he said merrily. "I brought your mom and grandma a little surprise."

She motioned for him to come in, and as he stepped inside, he noticed her tear-streaked cheeks and quiet demeanor.

He peeked into the living room to see her mother sitting there crying as well. Only her grandmother rose from her chair to greet him. "Tucker, how wonderful to see you."

"Everything all right?"

"Oh, it will be," Eleanor Kerrigan assured him. "Holly just gave us some sad news, that's all."

He swung a gaze back to Holly.

She clasped her hands in front of her. "It can wait."

Ignoring the cold sense of dread that had settled in his stomach, he asked "Are you sure?"

"Marian," Mrs. Kerrigan said, putting a hand to her daughter's shoulder. "Why don't we leave them alone a minute?"

Tucker watched as Marian McCall, still sobbing, fled the room.

He propped the tree in a corner. "I don't think I want to wait. What's going on?" A million thoughts flashed through his mind, from her being sick to someone having died. To her getting married—to someone else.

"Tucker, the reason I came home this weekend was," she paused, and let out a sob. "I never expected... and now..."

"Slow down," he said. "Does this have

something to do with why you were crying last night?"

She sniffled, pulled in a deep breath. "I've taken a job in Chicago."

The words hung awkwardly between them before the realization slammed into him so hard he stumbled back a step. "*Chicago*?" That was more than just a few hours down the Thruway. "That's nearly a thousand miles away, Hol."

"I know." She wrung her hands, then gave a little cry. "You have to understand. I was only coming here to tell Mom and Gran that I wouldn't be home for Christmas this year. I start my new job the day after."

"You might have mentioned it last night."

"I tried," she said, eyes shimmering with tears. "I told you I couldn't get involved right now."

"But you never said why." He realized he'd raised his voice. He had no right to yell at her. They'd never made plans or promises. Not together anyway.

"You never gave me time to say why," she reminded him. "Yes, I should have brought it up. But I got so caught up in being with you and the girls that—"

"Marry me." He couldn't believe he'd actually said it. It was probably the most impulsive thing he'd ever done. And stupid. There was no way she'd say yes.

"You don't really mean that."

"I love you, Holly. I don't want to lose you

again."

"We never had each other to lose. Not thirteen years ago and not now." She turned away from him. "This job may lead to the network position I've always wanted, this is what I've been working toward my entire career. Besides, I don't ever want to get married Tucker. Not even to you."

He flinched at her choice of words. "Why?"

"I won't go through what my mother did, being abandoned with a child to care for. I won't put myself through it, and I certainly won't put a child through it."

"I'm not like your father, Holly." Was she really comparing him to a man who could walk away from his family?

She folded her arms over her chest and rubbed briskly. "What if I gain the weight back? There's not a man alive who, when shown a picture of what I used to look like, would take that chance. And if something happened, and I did go back to looking like that—"

"Damn it, Holly, when are you going to forgive me for that lapse in character, for being a stupid seventeen-year-old? I'm not that boy anymore. I'm a man, and not the kind who'd leave his family or I wouldn't be raising two little girls on my own." He took a deep breath and blew it out, his anger dissolving into aching disappointment. He couldn't believe she thought so little of him. He turned toward the front door. "I'm not going anywhere, Hol. Ten years from now I'll still be living across the street from your grandmother."

"Please don't wait for me, Tucker. I'm not going to change my mind."

"I won't." He cleared his throat against a sudden aching. "But you're wrong about one thing."

She sniffled and faced him, eyes watery, nose red. "Wrong about what?"

"There is one man who would take that chance, Hol. Me."

He stepped out the door into the cold night.

Seven

"Greeting cards have all been sent, the Christmas rush is through..."

Karen Carpenter's soulful voice poured from the radio as Holly sat on the couch in her empty living room, surrounded by packing boxes. She had worked the last day at her job in Syracuse yesterday. Tomorrow, Christmas day, she would fly to Chicago. A realtor had already found her an apartment there and most of her things had been shipped. All that remained was the couch, which she'd sold to a friend, a radio, her suitcase, and her cat, Calvin, who would be flying out with her tomorrow.

And one lonely string of Christmas lights over the window.

But she hadn't hung them because of any real Christmas spirit. She'd hung them because they reminded her of Tucker. She stared up at the changing lights. With the snow falling heavily outside, it reminded her more than ever of the night they'd spent together.

The past month had been rough. Lots of teary phone calls home. It wasn't that she'd never been away from home for Christmas before, it was that she'd never gone so far away. But this was her chance to make a name for herself in a bigger market, and that kind of success was what she'd spent the last decade of her life chasing.

The fluffy grey tabby rose from the back of the sofa and jumped down to her lap. She reached to pet him.

For some reason, thoughts of her new job no longer filled her with the sense of satisfaction it once had. Something was lacking. She didn't have to look far to know what it was. She missed Tucker. And those two sweet little girls. And that damn town she'd always hated.

Where was he now? She checked her watch. A little past ten a.m. He was probably working. But was he thinking of her? Or had he found someone else and moved on?

With a meow, Calvin stepped from the couch onto her lap, butting her chin with his head.

"I made the right choice, didn't I? I've waited my whole life for this opportunity." She cuddled the cat close. "I can't just throw it away."

The cat purred and nudged her hand for more petting.

Melancholy washed over her as the song continued about missing your true love on Christmas Eve. By the time the last note was sung, Holly was crying and singing along "I wish I were with you." Tucker's face filled her mind, the anguish in his eyes when she'd seen him last. She'd never voiced her fears of abandonment aloud before. It was ridiculous, really, to think no one would ever really love her for herself. Love her enough not to leave her. Love her—period.

There is one man who'd take that chance, Hol. Me.

She reached for a box of tissues to dab at the hot tears spilling freely down her cheeks. "I had the best thing that's ever happened to me, and I just shoved it away," she sobbed. "I think I may have thrown away the wrong opportunity, Calvin."

The cat jumped down, either frightened by her wailing or not interested.

Could she really be in love with Tucker after only one weekend together? But he'd felt it, too. Maybe something magical had happened there among the over-ripe pumpkin and the spilled milk. The kind of gift fate only handed out this time of year. The kind of gift you didn't ignore.

She jumped to her feet, spilling wadded up tissues from her lap. "I've got to tell him I love him, too." She grabbed her cell phone and was about to dial his number, but stopped herself. "I shouldn't do this over the phone." She glanced out the window at the heavy snowfall. It was five hours to Castleford. Longer than that in this storm.

"I don't care."

She dropped a couple of scoops of food into the cat's bowl to hold him over, freshened his water and shoved on her boots and jacket.

"Wish me luck, Calv!" She grabbed her car keys and ran out the door.

****

The five hour drive from Syracuse to

Castleford took closer to ten. Several exits off the Thruway were closed and Holly had been forced to travel back roads for most of the way. She kept the radio tuned to the news so she'd know what roads to avoid and kept her mind busy by making plans.

She'd always lived well within her means. Despite the blow her professional reputation would take when she turned down the Chicago job, she should still have no trouble finding another. And she had enough money saved to live off of for several months, if it took that long. Sooner or later something would come up at a local station, something closer to home.

Home. If Tucker had moved on, met someone else, it would never feel that way again. But she'd still stay, hold her ground, just as he'd said, and keep the small town of Castleford, New York on the map for as long as possible. Even if it was a losing battle.

"If I get back there alive," she said aloud, breathing a sigh of relief as she spotted the familiar blue sign that read "Welcome to Castleford." One long country road to drive down and then she'd come to Main Street.

She gave a little cry as the car skidded on the slippery road and veered toward the next lane. She righted it, thankful for her anti-lock brakes, and with trembling fingers reached to switch off the radio so she could concentrate.

"You can do this, Hol. You're almost there now." She had just rounded the corner to turn onto Main Street when the car hit a patch of ice. It spun around once and landed with a gentle whump into a pile of snow that the plows had pushed up on the corner.

Shaking, she shifted into reverse and tried to back up. Nothing. She tried to go forward but the wheels only spun.

Finally, with a growl of frustration, she climbed out.

"Oh, damn..." she moaned when she saw that the car was good and truly stuck. It would take a truck to pull her out of that mess. Well, if nothing else came to mind when she saw him, she could always tell Tucker she was simply stopping by because she needed him to pull her car out. Neighbors did that sort of thing for each other, after all.

She shivered as the falling snow soaked her hair. Gran's home-made floppy brown hat was still in the back seat where she kept it so she reached in and put it on, but she'd run out without gloves and had only pulled on a lightweight jacket. Everything else was already en route to Chicago.

Folding her arms over her chest, she began to trudge down the snow-laden sidewalks of Main Street. Everything was closed at this time of night, but most of the businesses had left their Christmas lights on. As she passed by signs that read "Closed—have a Merry Christmas" she felt a warm glow build inside her. She used to think this town was hokey, but maybe it *was* a good place to raise a family. She stopped and stared at the blinking lights on the window of the diner. A tree trimmed with sparkling ornaments stood inside. A beautiful tree. "Bet I know where that came from," she murmured.

She hovered in the doorway a moment, taking a brief respite from the falling snow. She turned to face the other businesses and saw the glow of the lights up and down the street. Reds and blues and greens against the snow-draped landscape. It was beautiful.

It was home.

Moving out of the doorway and away from the sidewalks, she headed into the middle of the street. The snow was building up, and it was difficult to move, but feeling the need to hurry, she ran. It was more of a trot really, and it struck her that she felt a bit like George Bailey at the end of *It's A Wonderful Life*. Glad to be home. Uncaring if she was wet and cold, or that the snow was soaking her clothing where her jacket didn't cover.

She stopped in the middle of the street, knowing there was no one around to see her, and spread her arms wide. "Merry Christmas, Castleford," she cried. She turned a slow circle, laughing at her own foolishness, and broke into a run again. "Tucker," she called, despite the fact that he was still two blocks away. "I'm home!"

****

Business at the farm had trickled off early; only a few diehards still came to cut their trees on Christmas Eve day, so Tucker had closed up at five. Let the corner Christmas tree lots and super stores stay open til seven if they wanted, he had a family to get home to.

The sky was turning dark; it was nearly time to tuck Aspen and Sierra in and read *T'was the Night Before Christmas,* as he did every year. He should feel a sense of relief that the busy season was over and just enjoy his two little girls and the holiday, but he couldn't.

His house, at least, was filled with family; his mother and father were here for Christmas, and the smells he remembered from his boyhood drifted from the kitchen. Aspen and Sierra were in the kitchen with "Grammy" baking special gingerbread cookies to leave for Santa tonight.

Along with his parents, his two brothers and their wives and kids had stopped by. And so had his ex and her new husband, who were now officially snowed in. The girls were excited to have their mom with them for Christmas, and even if it wasn't exactly his idea of fun, he was glad for them. So his house, at long last, was packed to the rafters with family and warmth. Even if he didn't feel especially in the Christmas spirit this year.

The sense of loss he'd struggled with for weeks hadn't left him. It had been foolish to get wrapped up in feelings for Holly so soon, yet he hadn't been able to shake the sense that they belonged together.

Of course he'd spent too many sleepless nights torturing himself, looking up her Syracuse news channel's site on the internet and watching video casts of her reports over and over.

Between work and heartache, he knew he'd

lost a few pounds. His mother had been flashing worried glances his way all afternoon. But she wouldn't ask, would assume he was torn up over Kim being there with her new husband. Truth was, he liked the guy. Probably better than he liked Kim these days. And the two were good for each other, and he seemed to fill her need for material things in a way Tucker never could. Or wanted to.

His mother came into the dining room where he stood staring out the window at the snowfall. "Do you want me to stay with the girls while you go to Midnight mass with your brothers?"

"No thanks. I'll take the girls and go in the morning."

"I saw Marian McCall earlier today," his mother went on. "I guess her Holly won't be home this year, took some big job in Chicago."

He slid his hands into his pockets, wondering how he could get out of this conversation. "I heard."

"Nice girl, Holly."

"Yep."

"I guess she's changed a lot, but I still remember that pudgy little girl who used to light up like a Christmas tree whenever you were around."

He heaved a sigh. "I remember."

"Daddy, Daddy, look!" Aspen bounded into the room, an ornament dangling from her fingers. "It's a snow globe! Just like in Polar Express—only it hangs on the tree!"

He hoisted her on his hip and kissed her cheek, grateful for the interruption.

"Mommy got it for me."

"It's beautiful, baby." It had probably cost a small fortune. He kissed her cheek and made the appropriate sounds of being impressed by the ornament.

"Will you help me hang it on the tree? Somewhere high, where Santa can see it."

He carried her into the living room where a tree he'd been shaping all year stood proud and tall, covered in ornaments and twinkling lights. He hoisted her onto his shoulders. "How about right up there?"

She giggled and reached to hang the ornament. As she did so, a movement outside the window caught his eye. A group of people moving down the street, glowing candles in hand.

"Carolers!" Sierra cried, running up to peer out the window. "Can we go out and see them, Daddy?"

"I'll get some cocoa and cookies ready," his mother said.

Tucker walked with both girls to the front door and stepped out onto the porch as the group stopped in front of their house.

"*We wish you a Merry Christmas, we wish you a Merry Christmas…*"

Still holding Aspen in his arms, and Sierra by the hand, he stood there, trying to feel the holiday spirit, trying to remember the magic this night had held when he was a kid. Trying like hell to enjoy it for his kids' sake. And failing miserably.

As the carolers finished their song, his mother stepped out onto the porch.

"What a night to be out," she said, handing around a plate full of warm cookies and mugs of cocoa. "But thank you so much. That was beautiful."

"Sing another one!" Aspen chirped. "Sing Rudolph!"

The group cheerfully obliged and as the adults and children on the porch sang along, Tucker did, too, in another attempt to force the holiday spirit.

As they sang the last verse, he saw something at the far end of the street. Someone running.

"Now who would be out for a walk tonight?" his mother asked.

"Hard to say." But something pulled his gaze back to the lone figure. Whoever it was slipped and fell, but as they rose to their feet once more something held his gaze. It couldn't be... no, she was in Chicago by now.

"Tucker!" A voice echoed from halfway down the street.

A tingle moved through him. It couldn't be. Joy settled in his heart, like the warm glow of a candle in a window. He set Aspen on her feet and moved down the steps, well aware of the stares of his entire family and the carolers still gathered on the front porch.

"Tucker!" she called again, close enough this time that he could see it was really her. Bedraggled, soaking wet, shivering. But it was

Holly.

He ran, feet slipping on the heavy snow and ice and met her as she ran toward him.

She let out a cry and slipped. He reached a hand out and pulled her up.

"Oh, Tucker," she said, voice quivering from cold. "I was so stupid."

"I thought you were in Chicago." He placed his hands to her cold cheeks and stared into her face. "What are you doing here?"

"I'm coming home."

"For Christmas?"

"No." She shook her head. "To stay."

He let out a whoop of delight and twirled her around in his arms.

"My—my car is stuck in the snow a couple blocks back, and everything I own is on the way to Chicago. My cat is still at home in Syracuse, I have to go back for him but... "She met his gaze, looking a little frightened. "I love you Tucker. Please say I'm not too late."

"You're not."

Right there in the snow he dropped to one knee, uncaring that it was cold and wet and they were both shivering and covered in snow. A gasp of delight went up from the family gathered on his front porch, and from her mother and grandmother, who had come out onto theirs. "Marry me, Holly."

"Yes," she said, shivering.

"Tonight," he said, rising to his feet and scooping her into his arms. He carried her down the street and toward the sidewalk that led to his house. *Their* house.

Sierra and Aspen bounded down the steps with a squeal. "Holly!"

Tucker stopped and gazed into her face. "I don't want to spend another Christmas without you."

"You won't," she vowed, pressing her cold lips to his. "I promise."

He rested his forehead against hers. "Aw, Holly," he said, fighting back tears of happiness. "What made you change your mind?"

"Oh, just some Christmas lights." She shrugged. "And the promise of a small town Christmas. With you."